Praise for
Next Year in Jerusalem!

"An entertaining read set in a magical city, heightened by a combination of psychological insights, spiritual ponderings and suspense elements."

Sandra Levy Ceren, PhD, Author of the Dr Cory Cohen Mystery Series

"I traveled to Israel vicariously with Natalie and Maggie and enjoyed each step along the cobbled streets of ancient Jerusalem. Barbara Becker Holstein weaves themes of friendship, love, spirituality, and mystery, engaging the reader from the start. I can't wait for Part 2!"

Kate Grady

"What I loved about this book is that I related to it so well. I could see myself with my two best friends doing exactly what these women were doing, traveling and being in Jerusalem. Also, the romance, mystery and the spiritual, were a combination I thoroughly enjoyed. I just kept reading and reading. I can't wait for book #2. You've got to read *Next Year in Jerusalem*, Part I, so you can read Part 2!"

Rosemary DeSarno

Next Year in Jerusalem!

NEXT YEAR
IN
JERUSALEM!

Around Every Corner, Mystery &
Romance in the Holy Land

Part Two

Dr. Barbara Becker Holstein

ISBN: 978-0-9798952-4-1 (Paperback)
        978-0-9798952-5-8 (eBook, ePub)

Book design by Five Rainbows Services
www.FiveRainbows.com

In memory of my mother, Bernice Silverman Becker (1920-2010), who infused me with love and a sense of the romance and mystery of life. She gave me the courage to use my imagination, to tell my dreams, and to be certain that despite any stormy days, the sun will always come out tomorrow.

To my husband, Russell Holstein, Ph.D., the love of my life, my best friend and my bedrock. With Russell at my side, so many of my dreams have come true!

To my dear friend Susan Weiner, who sat with me at lunch on a summer day when the plot of this book was born and written on paper napkins. The story came through our fingertips as clearly as if we were being guided from above. *Next Year In Jerusalem!* had announced itself and there was only one choice: to start writing. And so I did.

Natalie and Maggie, best friends since college, find themselves in Jerusalem when Natalie's husband, David, takes a short sabbatical there. Intrigued by a mystery woman, Chaya Sarah, both women are soon captivated by spiritual and traditional religious experiences she offers them. However, they are also baffled by some of her actions and her secrecy about herself and begin to feel that Chaya Sarah may be involved in more than meets the eye, perhaps she is even in danger.

The mystical energy of Jerusalem along with the reality of terrorism compounds an already intense experience for both women. Their emotions are heightened further when Natalie's old boyfriend, Jack, reappears and insists in taking them all out on the town. Danger lurks as Natalie's husband has to be away in Haifa the very night that Jack is taking them out. Natalie is surprised that night by the intensity of her feelings for Jack. She realizes she is close to a decision that she may soon regret.

Maggie, divorced and involved in a new romance in Manhattan, finds herself intrigued and aroused by Jack's colleague Raji, a tall, dark and handsome stranger. As Part 1 concludes, the plot can only thicken!

The End of Part 1

If time could stop, it would have, as Jack's eyes obviously begged an invitation to come upstairs.

Should Natalie let him? Should she respond to her newly revived feelings and Jack's yearnings? *Take me in. Hold me. Fall asleep in my arms*...the message she had answered so many times before with a *yes*. She reminded herself that David was away for the night. No one would ever know, except Maggie. That wasn't true. She would know, even if David never found out. No amount of passionate love making was worth breaking the trust between them. She glanced at Maggie and Raji who, exuberant and upbeat, were exchanging e-mail addresses and cell phone numbers. Animation and energy ran between them in a free-flow. They both looked as fresh as if the day had just begun.

The elevator arrived. Jack gave Natalie one more longing look and a last tender kiss. Natalie blushed as if she'd been seen by a thousand on-lookers. "I'll talk to you tomorrow," Jack murmured. She didn't answer. Her answer had already been given, and this time it was a *no*.

A glowing Maggie laughed and pushed in beside her as the doors closed. "You sure are awake," Natalie noted. "I've never seen you this fresh and alive after seven p.m.!"

"Raji energizes me the way no one else ever has. There's such a lightness about him that's not silly or trivial. Maybe after that maniac husband of mine who screamed at everyone and everything and managed to criticize me for even being alive, I'm just so responsive to normal guys. Gary is totally normal also, but he doesn't have the same interests as me. I'm not saying we don't manage to have fun. But Raji is magical."

"Just remember, you don't really know him yet. Magical people can also be illusionists."

"Oh, Natalie, you're just trying to tame me and protect me. But don't worry. After all, we go home the day after tomorrow. So maybe I'll just have one more day of fun. And then our lives will be back to what they were. Well, probably, anyway."

Maggie turned her attention to her friend. "And what about you? What the hell were you doing holding Jack's hand and letting him treat you like his girl, almost thirty years after the last time you've seen him? What don't I know? Where were the two of you, shopping in galleries or necking in a dark alley?"

Natalie blushed almost scarlet, even through her exhaustion. "Ah, I see, my intuition was correct!" Maggie continued, relentless. "Was it good? Did you want more? What in the world are you thinking? What about David?"

The elevator arrived at their floor. "I don't know," Natalie answered. "I just don't know!"

And now, *Next Year in Jerusalem*, Part 2

Chapter One

Instantly Natalie saw the red light on the room phone, signaling a voice mail. Who could be calling her? Her kids had her cell number. David already talked to her. There were three messages.

"Hi, Honey, it's midnight." David's voice sounded loving and caring. "I thought you would be back by now. I just called to say I miss you."

Second message: "Where are you?" David's voice sounded slightly edgy, but still affectionate and light. "It's one o'clock and you're not answering your cell phone. What, did you run out on me with your old flame? Call me."

Third message: "Where are you?" Now he sounded worried and almost angry. "It's one forty-five and you still haven't called me back! What in the world happened to your cell? I'm concerned!"

"Oh my G-d, why didn't my cell phone ring?" Natalie began to panic. "I didn't notice a message light."

She grabbed her cell and found that it was turned off. She realized instantly that, in the chaos of the restaurant and the belly dancer gyrating, she'd accidentally turned her phone off instead of just hitting the end key when she said goodbye to David.

Now she was in a mess! Her heart pounded and she was perspiring as she called David's cell.

"Hello," a sleepy voice answered.

"Hi, David, I'm so sorry, I accidentally turned off my cell at the restaurant." *No lie there!*

"What the hell were you doing out so late?" David had recovered quickly from his grogginess. "I was really scared."

"We sat outside on Ben Yuhuda Street and people-watched. We also went into a few galleries." *Again, no lie*, Natalie thought.

"Into the wee hours of the morning?"

"As we were walking to the car, something was going on down a side street, and we stopped to watch."

"What kind of something?"

"We couldn't tell, maybe a terrorist attack or something way down the street. They had it barricaded." *Wow, I got this far in total honesty,* Natalie marveled. *Well, not really total honesty...but at least not full disclosure.*

"I was really worried, and there was a little part of me that was jealous." David's voice softened. "After all, Jack was a long time boyfriend before I came along."

"Oh, honey, and how many years have we been married?"

"Over twenty-five."

"That means you forget exactly how many. Maybe it's my turn to be concerned."

They laughed, and the tension disappeared as if it had never existed.

"I'll be home tomorrow night," David told her. I'll have an early supper with my hosts and then come back to Jerusalem and to the hotel room by ten, so we can pack. I assume you'll be waiting for me when I get back? No night on the town tomorrow night, please?"

"Of course I'll be waiting. I have a massage at six at the hotel spa, and then Maggie and I will have a bite to eat in the hotel."

"I love you."

"I love you, too."

"Good night!"

"Sleep tight."

"Don't let the bedbugs bite."

Natalie put the phone down, relieved but still in turmoil. David was such a sweetheart. He had an innocence and trust that made her dilemma that much more scary. She started to undress and take off her make-up when she heard a text alert.

David never sent texts. She knew even before she picked up her phone that it was Jack.

Chapter Two

"Miss you already, see you tomorrow?"

Natalie didn't answer. She couldn't. She was too exhausted. But she used her last bit of energy to hide the bracelet Jack bought her. Better she shouldn't be wearing it. She didn't want to lie to David that she bought it for herself and she didn't want to tell the truth. She wrapped it up inside a pair of pantyhose, took one last look as she fingered the dainty sterling links and rubbed the ancient glass that glowed in the light of the bedroom lamp. Then she hid the pantyhose in the side pouch of her suitcase. Finally, Natalie fell into bed, put one pillow over her eyes and tried to go to sleep.

In another room nearby, Maggie had no trouble relaxing and falling asleep. Even though both Raji and Gary had already texted her, she felt at peace. Her husband had been a cheat and no good. She wasn't married and she hadn't betrayed anyone. As she lay in bed she thought of Gary, enjoying her warm feelings for him.

She had slept with Gary, and if she now proceeded to sleep with Raji, it would definitely complicate her life for a while. But she didn't feel she was doing an injustice to Gary at this point. They had no commitment to each other, and if she was going to end up as anyone's wife, she knew that she needed to get her bearings straight with men and with life.

Yes, Gary was charming in an American way. He was grounded and good-hearted. He was Jewish and savvy about Jewish politics and Israel, and enjoyed living a Jewish style of life, which meant bagels and lox on Sundays, celebrating major Jewish holidays, and being totally comfortable with Jewish schtick. Also, he was a detective and she loved his knowledge of how one goes about solving crimes or figuring out mysteries. And she couldn't wait to talk to him about Chaya Sarah in detail when she got home.

As sleep began to overcome her, Maggie also thought about Raji. She couldn't wait to really get to know him. Maybe that meant "knowing" in the Biblical sense. She laughed to herself as she remembered a rabbi saying that "knowing" was a modest way of indicating sexual relationships. But maybe it just meant friendship. Oh, well, whatever it turned out to be, Raji was just so amazing. He epitomized the tall, dark, handsome foreigner, and she couldn't resist that allure.

By comparison, Raji's charms were much more blatant than Gary's. He was mannerly in a way that most American guys just aren't. He was interested in every word that came out of her mouth. Gary had a kind of sincerity but lacked the level of eye contact and concentration that Raji displayed. Raji liked the same things that she did, which was utterly amazing to her. She thought that no man in the world could possibly like all the eclectic topics in life that appealed to her, unless he was gay. And Raji obviously wasn't gay! She could feel his raw manliness beneath the external charm and polish...feel it as if it was sending heat waves into her very being, from her head to her toes.

Gary was fine, but he wasn't sending out that kind of sexual energy, even during sex itself. She hadn't known that level existed, except in fantasy or in the mystique of historical icons. She'd always imagined that King Solomon with his hundreds of wives had that kind of sexual radiance.

Almost asleep now, Maggie sighed, thinking, *I can't wait for tomorrow, a day with Raji to finish my trip to Israel! I can't believe my good fortune.*

Natalie still tossed and turned at five o'clock in the morning. She must have been dreaming, because she was sweating and thought she'd just received a text on her cell phone from Batyag. *Natalie, how are you? Let's make a plan. Cheap flights to Africa right now.*

She lay in bed and told herself that no matter how inexpensive the flight, she couldn't go because she had to return home to Connecticut. She had a life, and why the hell had Batyag taken so many years to get in touch? It took a minute to realize that she'd been dreaming.

She got up, reached for a washcloth and wet it. She lay down again and placed the cloth across her forehead. It was soothing and just the type of cure her mother suggested whenever she had a restless night as a little girl.

Sleep finally came, just four hours, but enough to allow her to function. By ten a.m., she knew what she would text back to Jack.

Chapter Three

Natalie took a long shower after she texted Jack. She scrubbed her skin with chocolate sugar crystals and applied a short facemask of Israeli mud from the Dead Sea. She donned a beautiful long black and white sundress she'd purchased the week before but hadn't worn yet. The dress had a black background with large white petal flowers. The neckline was scooped and the skirt flared slightly coming down almost to her ankles.

They ate brunch on the hotel patio at eleven, and Natalie and Maggie looked amazingly fit and pretty considering their late night.

"Natalie you look stunning!" Maggie decided she loved the word "stunning" because it fit some occasions so perfectly. "I thought you'd be up half the night and a mess today."

"I was up half the night, and more," Natalie confirmed. "But by morning I'd made a decision."

"And what, may I ask, is your decision?"

"I'm not seeing Jack today—I texted him this morning that I'll be busy all day. I'm going to see Chaya Sarah."

Again the sound of a text rang out.

"Natalie, your phone."

"I'm ignoring it. David doesn't text."

"And what will you do when you get home and Jack is still texting you?"

"I may have to ask him to stop."

Maggie's eyes suddenly lost their early morning twinkle. "Are you really ready to do that? I saw a look in your eyes last night that I haven't seen in a long time."

Natalie looked away into the horizon. "You're right. Just because I'm not seeing him today doesn't mean I've fully processed what happened last night."

"Maybe Chaya Sarah can give you some advice," Maggie suggested as the waiter placed scrambled eggs and toast on the table. "She seems very wise."

"Yeah, maybe, but really I'm going back to see her because I don't want to leave without knowing more about who she is and what her life is all about. I don't want to leave another mystery in my life unanswered. Are you coming with me?"

"No, I have plans with Raji," Maggie said. "But tell her 'hello' and 'good-bye' for me, in case we don't see her again before we leave. I would come with you, but I'm just too intrigued with Raji. I trust you to find out the truth."

"Okay, see you back here at seven-thirty for some supper," Natalie agreed.

"Maybe...if I'm not back, I'm still with Raji. Don't worry. I'll be back by midnight, I promise."

"Okay. Have fun," Natalie said somewhat wistfully. She wished she could see a way out of her dilemma. As good as she felt when she'd walked into breakfast was how badly she felt now. She realized that Maggie was her voice of reason and truth. As soon as Maggie spoke and questioned what had seemed a completely easy decision a short while ago, she realized how far she was from a clear brain and decision. Maybe Chaya Sarah would have some thoughts on the matter.

Natalie remembered when she was small and her parents had some sort of problem. Maybe it was about finances. She wasn't sure. But off they all went to Aunt Molly's house. She and her sisters played in the basement while her parents talked to Aunt Molly. When they left they looked so relaxed and relieved. "No one is as wise as Aunt Molly," her dad commented in the car. "It's a special gift to be able to listen and give good advice."

Chaya Sarah had that special gift.

Chapter Four

The walk to Chaya Sarah's school seemed long and lonely. Not having Maggie with her was a letdown. She hadn't realized how much she relied on her friend for comfort and conversation. Walking alone wasn't the same. She felt as if her whole body was dragging.

She barely noticed the transition as she moved from the secular neighborhoods into the religious area. Her head was too full of her own emotions to hear or notice the ambulances that sped by. Nor did she see the barricaded side street that had been open to traffic the last time she'd passed it.

She hadn't even bothered to look at any of the newspapers today. If she had, she would've read about the suicide bomber who blew herself up just a few blocks from Ben Yuhuda Street late the previous night. Fortunately, only three passersby were injured, but not seriously. Most disturbing about the suicide bombing, and the reason the article appeared in the newspapers, was the fact that the suicide bomber had been another woman meticulously dressed as a religious Jew, complete with religious garb from dark stockings to a wig, psalm book in hand. She appeared to be about forty years old.

Still oblivious, Natalie finally approached the girls' school. It had started to drizzle, but fortunately she had an umbrella with her, as she'd heard a forecast of showers. She glanced at the school, and didn't notice the absence of lovely young voices chanting from the open windows. Nor did she notice the closed windows and the fact that there was no light shining from within.

Natalie remained totally in her own head as she walked around to the back of the building. The door opened immediately. Had she been more focused, she undoubtedly would have wondered if she'd actually knocked on the door before it opened. As if by magic, she was welcomed by Chaya Sarah.

Chaya Sarah, the same warm and effusive woman, folded Natalie into her arms for a generous hug. Natalie began to cry. Chaya Sarah stepped back and took her by the arm.

"Come, sit down," she comforted Natalie. "Please make yourself at home. I just made some mint tea. I'll get you some; it's in the other room. Sit and I'll be right back. Then we can talk. I have lots of time."

Chaya Sarah stepped out of the little office into the shadows, and quickly reappeared holding a china teapot, two delicate teacups, and a package of cream cookies.

Natalie sniffed and cried a bit, as she clutched a small wad of tissues.

Chaya Sarah bustled about, poured the tea, opened the package of cookies, and moved the Kleenex box closer to Natalie. Somehow, she managed to exude just the right amount of tender loving care and attention without invading Natalie's space.

Chaya Sarah was like the best mother she'd never had, Natalie thought. The personification of a devoted mother figure, calm, caring, and totally accepting without being overbearing, she acted the way her own mother had, on occasion.

Chaya Sarah was so perfectly in tune with her. She didn't ask a million questions, she was just there, quiet and ready for whenever and however Natalie needed her. Time didn't matter. In fact, Natalie began to feel that nothing mattered very much, even before she began to pour out her troubled heart. Once Chaya Sarah listened to her story, she instinctively knew that everything would be all right. She intuited, even before she started, that Chaya Sarah would know what Natalie should do.

Natalie could feel herself less intensely stressed as she felt bathed in a loving gaze. How wonderful to be Chaya Sara's only concern for the moment.

As Natalie slowly sipped the restorative mint tea, her stress lessened. Wasn't this what they'd drunk last night in the restaurant? She hadn't had mint tea the entire trip, until last night and today. Oh, well, so what? The important thing was that her breathing had become less rapid and she felt safe and so understood, even before she uttered a word.

Now ready to tell her story, tell it she did, from last evening when Jack and Raji drove up in the limousine, to her husband's anger when she wasn't back at the hotel, to her resolution this morning not to answer Jack's texts. She left out only the part where she and Jack had walked down the alley and kissed. *Not lies, just some omissions*, she told herself. After all, a person like Chaya Sarah wouldn't want to hear those kinds of details. She was too pure.

Chaya Sarah sat quietly after Natalie finished her story. Finally she asked, "do you have any intention of leaving your husband?"

"Oh no, of course not! I love David very much."

"Do you see him as your soul mate?"

"What do you mean?" Natalie asked.

"Do you value him as the person with whom you have built a life? Someone with whom you've climbed some mountains and trudged through some valleys, and know each other's personal pains as well as joys?"

"He's always been there for me," Natalie acknowledged. "When I had my miscarriage at five months, he was by my side holding me and promising that things would be all right, that there would be another baby. We've laughed and cried together over the kids, and lived through both of them having enough problems as teens to want to pull our hair out. So I guess the answer is *yes*."

"Could you conceive of hurting him by leaving him for another man?"

"No, never!"

Then why is there such a fire in me, Natalie thought as she answered Chaya Sarah's questions.

"So what you are really telling me is that you *do* see David as your life partner," Chaya Sarah stated. "I think I have a good idea what will help free you from the extra emotions you experienced last night."

Natalie's face brightened. "What?"

"Have you ever been to a mikvah?" Chaya Sarah asked.

Natalie was stunned. What in the world did that have to do with what had happened, or with the discussion they'd just been having about whether she and David were soul mates?

"A mikvah? No, never."

"Then you may not realize that a mikvah is one of the ways that G-d has given us to sanctify marriage?"

"I didn't realize that. My grandmother told us that after she came to America she never went to the mikvah again. There was no reason to, since her apartment had a tub. I always thought it was a way to get clean, before people had their own bathrooms."

"No. A mikvah is a way to purify oneself in a special way. By entering the purest of waters and totally immersing yourself, you connect with G-d in a unique way. You probably didn't know that brides go to the mikvah before they marry, not just in the middle of the month."

"No, I didn't know that. No one in my family ever went to the mikvah."

"A married woman, no matter what her age, whether she is able to have children anymore or not, can still go to the mikvah once as if she is a bride. After that, she should go every month when her cycle is over. However, even if she no longer has a cycle she can still be a bride once. It is a lovely tradition for those women who never had a chance to go. Maybe you would like to go. It might be a way to really reconnect with your husband and with yourself."

Natalie was totally blown away. She'd expected some sort of analysis of last night, along with some appropriate advice. Instead Chaya Sara was encouraging her to step into pure water and get her head entirely wet. This was supposed to help? How?

"I-I don't know what to say," Natalie stammered. "But I do know that I want to feel at peace again. I can't stand the turmoil I felt before I got here."

"I think this would help. Let me tell you more about what you would do. And, by the way, you can do it tonight."

"Tonight? Here in Jerusalem?"

"Yes, no problem. Actually, here in Jerusalem we have some of the most beautiful mikvahs in the world. I can call one of them for you and make an appointment. You would go at sundown. A matron will be there to meet you and explain how to prepare yourself. Then she will take you into the mikvah and remain there to lead you in several short prayers. And you can also take some time alone in the purifying waters. By the time you come home to your husband you will feel really close to him and eager to have relations. It is a mitzvah to make love after coming back from the mikvah. Shall I call and make an appointment for you?"

Natalie's head reeled, yet she found herself saying, "sure, I guess so."

Chaya Sarah took a business card from a small pile on her desk. "Here, I have some cards from the Pure Waters Mikvah. Take one. You will probably need to take a taxi from the hotel. Just give the card to the driver. And remember to arrive after sundown."

"Will they know why I'm coming there?"

"Of course. I'll be calling them for you."

"Tomorrow night we go home. Maybe Maggie and I can come by tomorrow and see you for a few minutes?"

Chaya Sarah had turned away to answer her cell phone. Natalie recognized the look of concern on her face as Chaya Sarah turned away from her. It had been there the last visit too, when she'd also gotten a phone call. Once again a foreign language replaced Chaya Sarah's fine English. Exactly what language was it? Natalie still wasn't sure. She wanted to ask, but Chaya Sarah finished the phone call and told Natalie, "I must take care of some matters."

"But you'll call for me? I don't want to show up in a strange place and no one knows why I'm there."

"Don't worry," Chaya Sarah reassured her. "I'll call."

Before Natalie knew what had happened, they hugged quickly and she found herself out on the street once again. It was already late afternoon. She must have been there for hours! Amazing!

Natalie realized once again that she hadn't asked even one of the questions about Chaya Sarah she'd promised herself to ask.

Chapter Five

It stopped raining, the late afternoon sun was shining, and the air smelled fresh.

Natalie started to walk, her mind in a whirl. Her emotional state was calmer, and she realized she'd committed herself to a new adventure that she wasn't at all sure she really wanted to take. Dunking in a mikvah? What was she thinking? Wait until Maggie heard this one! But, at the same time there was a part of her, deep down, that was ready for this new adventure; ready to climb mountains to be purified and feel comfortable with David again.

Natalie heard a "ding" from her phone, indicating a text. She assumed it was from Jack and was prepared not to answer it. But still she had to look. It could be from Maggie. She hailed a passing cab, settled in, and checked. It was from Jack. She couldn't help reading it: *You are my soul mate. Need to talk.*

She thought, *soul mate? After more than twenty-five years of being out of touch? After not caring how I felt if I'd been pregnant when we were together? And only caring about yourself! After marrying someone else and having three kids? Soul mates? You hadn't climbed one single mountain for me or with me.*

Natalie found herself getting so angry and as she stepped out of the taxi back at the hotel she said under her breath, "I'll show him who my soul mate is! I'm going to the mikvah and I'm going to enjoy every minute, even if I get water in my ears when I dunk."

Another text, this time from Maggie. *Go ahead and eat without me. I'm spending my last night in Jerusalem with Raji. What a delicious, wonderful day we had, can't wait to share. How about you? See you at breakfast.*

Natalie was actually relieved Maggie was out. She wanted to talk to her, but she also wanted to be by herself until the mikvah thing was over and she could process the experience a little. Everything was happening too fast to even find delight in sharing it with Maggie. And thankfully she didn't have to tell David yet, as he wasn't coming home until around ten o'clock. She was sure she'd be back from the mikvah by then. So here she was, her last night in Jerusalem, about to do something supposedly "purifying."

Natalie grabbed a quick bite at the bar area of the hotel, cancelled her massage, and went up to her room to change before getting a cab to the mikvah. Suddenly, she experienced a great urge to undress and take a shower. She threw her clothes on the floor and looked at her naked body in the full-length mirror. It was strange to come so close to her physical self, when she was trying so hard to get a hold on her emotional self. Yet in a way that was what the mikvah was all about. You stood stark naked to elevate your soul.

Refreshed by the shower, by the time she left to hail a cab Natalie felt very excited. *I'm having my own private adventure! David will think I'm out of my mind, but I don't care.*

Natalie handed the taxi driver the mikvah's business card.

"I guess that is a new one," the driver commented. "I don't know the place, but I know the street. We'll find it. Do you want to stop at the Wall on the way? We're going right by it. A lot of people like to stop, especially at sunset."

"Sure, why not? I'm up for anything tonight!"

"What did you say, lady?"

"Yes. Let's stop."

A few minutes later Natalie walked toward the women's side of the Wall. The sun was setting, and behind the Wall the sky turned a soft purple. The air was still extremely fresh from the rain. She inhaled deeply.

As she approached the Wall a number of haggard looking older women held up red strings. Several actually tied some on her wrist before she could stop them. In broken English they kept making remarks like, "string is good luck. Keep string on. No take off! Many miracles!"

Soon she'd distributed dollar bills to three different ladies. Three red strings were enough. She pushed past the next five and made her way to the Wall.

Natalie rubbed the stones with her hands. She closed her eyes and absorbed the energy of them, still warm from the day's sun.

It was a quick visit. Nothing amazing happened, but it did feel comforting to stop at the Wall, almost like an old friend who's heard your story before, but never minds hearing it again.

She spotted her taxi and continued on her way to the mikvah.

She noticed several messages and texts. David had checked in and indicated he might be back a little late, maybe not until ten-thirty. Natalie was relieved, since she didn't know how long the mikvah procedure would take. "See you then. Miss you," his voice had soothed.

There were three texts from Jack. She didn't answer any of them. He was trying to woo her with memories of past times. *Remember the night we stayed in the Catskills at that awful hotel where the mouse ran across the bedroom floor?* And, *remember the time we went ice-skating on the Charles River?*

I'm not even reading the third one, she thought. She deleted them, as if that would somehow cut the old ties that still lingered just beneath the surface of her present life. His insistence wasn't fair. Tonight was for Natalie and David. It was a validation of their status as soul mates. What right did Jack have to interfere? What business did he have being so damn arousing? What curse was on her cells that made them so responsive to his body?

Natalie was soon interrupted by the taxi driver who, delighted to have an English-speaking customer, told her he'd lived in Los Angeles for five years with his mother's brother. He took great pleasure in sharing his politics while practicing his English skills, he added.

Natalie learned all his views on the current government in Israel (it should step down); the tax system (over fifty percent of his income went to his taxes, he was drowning), and the cost of housing and food (which in his opinion were nightmares). How was anyone expected to make a living in this country? The rich got richer and the poor got poorer.

"Here we are, ma'am." They pulled up in front of a plain stucco one-story building. The only windows were small, high up, and covered with shades. The number 734 was prominent on the door, but there was no name on the building.

The taxi driver commented, "Strange neighborhood for a mikvah. Usually they're near synagogues or in religious neighborhoods. We're almost on the East Jerusalem border here. This neighborhood has some Israeli Arab families and some very secular Jewish families, people who want to show they can live in harmony. The rest of us know we can't!

"Listen, do you want me to wait for you? I'd be happy to. I wouldn't want to drop my wife off here and just leave."

"No, I don't know how long I'll be." Natalie thought it would seem creepy to have a man she'd never met wait while she stood naked in a pool of pure water. "Give me your card, and I'll call your taxi service when I'm done."

"Okay, Lady. I'll be on until eleven o'clock."

Chapter Six

As the driver pulled away, Natalie realized how poorly lit the street was. Now, well past dusk, the one street light way down the block did nothing to brighten the end where she stood. The building itself had one little light above the doorway. As she walked along the sidewalk to the front door, she shivered suddenly and wondered why in the world she'd sent away her protection?

She rang the bell. Immediately a sweet young woman, probably no more than twenty-nine or thirty, head kerchief neatly in place, answered the door. Natalie felt better. Now to introduce herself and get started. Her heart pounded, but from excitement, not fear.

"Can I help you?"

"Chaya Sarah made an appointment for me to come here tonight after sundown."

"Oh, sorry, phones no working," the girl said in broken English. "No messages this week."

Natalie felt her heart begin to pound harder. Now she was upset. Another mix-up, another confusion where she would never know if Chaya Sarah had tried to call!

"Oh, well, I'm here to go into the mikvah. I understand I can go in as a bride, even though I've been married many years. It is my first time. I was told a matron would show me what to do and give me a prayer to say."

"First time? No problem. Come in. I will show you where to go. Cost ninety shekels. Fill out form."

Natalie handed over the money, and signed the visitor sheet (a blank piece of notepaper with the date at the top). She was not at all sure the young woman understood most of what she said. Only later did she wonder why she so freely signed a blank piece of paper with her name and full home address.

"Come this way." The young woman led Natalie past a small waiting room with pleasant pink walls and a soft gray marble floor. There were no pictures, no signs and no literature with the facility's name. The place was stark, but certainly clean and feminine in its color scheme. It was eerily quiet. Natalie wished she had asked the taxi driver to wait.

The young woman spoke. "Please, you go here," she said as she opened the door of a large, attractive bathroom with many mirrors. "Robe in there," she explained as she pointed to a small closet. "After shower, go down hall to mikvah."

"Will you be coming in to help me?" Natalie practically begged. "Are there prayers to say?"

"See, mikvah down there. You open and go in. No one bother you."

Obviously, they hadn't communicated clearly. "Any prayers to say?" Natalie tried one more time.

The young woman looked perplexed. "Mrs. Levy not here, I alone." It hadn't seemed to work, and eventually Natalie realized that not only was the woman's English poor, but apparently Mrs. Levy was the wisdom keeper of everything, including the prayers. Finally, she surmised that she'd have to make the most of her experience. So much for that; she'd just have to carry on by herself. There was no going back now.

The woman walked back to the desk in the waiting room and sat down. Apparently, it was all now in Natalie's hands.

She went into the bathroom and started to undress. Determined to make the most of this situation, she let the environment begin to take over. This was going to be fun. Yes, she would prepare for the mikvah as if she was a Queen. Maybe she'd been the Queen of Sheba in another life? She laughed to herself, and then the image of being a very special bride on her wedding night came to her. It was a lovely image.

Somehow the environment elicited from her vague yet powerful feelings. She felt so female, part of a special group, a sisterhood of women who had gone from babyhood to elder years...one by one in an endless chain of family life, belonging to the same tribe. She saw her body today, naked in the mirrors, and once more felt moved to tears. She envisioned those before her—her grandmothers and her mother, and then saw her daughter after her, and imagined granddaughters in the future. She felt their energy, their hopes, dreams and prayers along with hers in the highly charged feminine bathroom.

She felt good although she was crying at the same time. The golden chain of women in her mind's eye engaged in no gossip, put-downs, criticisms or comparisons. It was as if each woman had been branded with a primitive imprint that identified them as belonging to the same clan. No need for words. Just timeless knowledge, maybe first known by Eve in the

Garden of Eden and passed down over hundreds of generations, a knowledge of mannerisms and hopes and dreams that transcended time. And now she stood right here in the midst of it, finally able to enjoy the same rights as other Jewish women throughout history.

Natalie showered again with a vengeance. She was determined to be as clean as she could be for the purifying waters. With no one to guide her, she washed her hair, took off her make-up, and trimmed her nails with the small scissor that lay on the vanity. She looked at the three red strings on her wrist. Should she leave them? It didn't seem right, since she knew she was to be completely unadorned. Without another thought she cut them off with the scissor.

She was ready now. She took a fluffy robe from the closet, and a pair of paper slippers, the kind they give you when you're in the hospital. She also grabbed a towel from the closet shelf and proceeded down the hall.

The building was totally silent. When she looked back she didn't even see the young woman in the waiting room any more. She could see from the small window in the hallway that it was pitch dark outside. The only noise was that of a siren somewhere, and the sound of an occasional car passing by.

She opened the door to the mikvah. The room was the size of a small bedroom with white tile walls, and most of it was taken up by what looked like a very small swimming pool. She'd feared the water would be cold, but as she stepped down a small staircase into the water, she was surprised as the pleasant warmth rushed up to her. At chest level the water seemed so much smoother and silkier than regular water. She sank down further, letting her hands float at her sides as the water welcomed her. A profound feeling of safety and calmness enveloped her. Were there guardian angels in here with her? It felt that way, but she wasn't scared. She felt protected and loved and, in turn, felt her heart opening up toward David.

Making her own prayer she said aloud softly, "Dear G-d, may David and I be blessed with the harmony that comes from being soul mates. And may I have the strength not to be influenced by other forces not in my best interests."

That covered it. She wasn't going to credit Jack by even saying his name aloud in these sacred waters.

She dunked herself in the waters three times, really fast. She had promised herself, but that part was hard. She grasped her towel and wiped her eyes and ears. She had almost drowned on Cape Cod once as a child, but a big strong man had pulled her out. Since then, she could never stand to go underwater. But this time it was worth it. This was for their marriage and for herself.

She returned to her changing room where she took another shower, this time a quick one, and got dressed. When she went back to the waiting room no one was there. In fact the young woman never reappeared even when Natalie called out.

Chapter Seven

Now it was getting creepy again. She called the taxi service on her cell. Within ten minutes a taxi appeared. It
wasn't the same driver. Natalie got in and gave the name
of her hotel. Not a word was exchanged. Twenty minutes later they drove by the Wall, which was lit up and
still busy. She remembered the women telling her not to
take the red strings off. "String is good luck. Keep string
on. No take off! Many miracles!" She also realized that
not only had she cut them off, she'd left them back at the
mikvah. Still high from her experience, she told herself
it didn't matter, it was nonsense, just superstition, like
the "evil eye" and saying "pooh-pooh".

Back at her hotel five minutes later, it was only nine-
thirty and David had not yet returned. Apparently Maggie
had, and desperately wanted to chat. *Knock on my door as
soon as you're back,* she'd texted.

Natalie knocked.

Maggie was beaming as she opened the door and
practically dragged her friend through it. "I had the
most incredible day! How was yours?"

"Great. The mikvah was amazing. I felt so special and connected and ready to be with David, my soul mate."

Maggie cut her off, obviously filled to the brim with news and excitement. "Good. I'm glad it was so uplifting. Someday I will dunk! But right now, Raji is amazing! I might be falling in love. Come sit on the bed with me. I have to tell you about the whole day!

"First Raji took me to this great pancake house where we ate brunch, pancakes, yogurt, fresh fruit, cheeses and the most amazing coffee cake I've ever tasted! And some kind of babka that's won awards in Israel. The coffee was so delicious! Some guy hand picks the coffee beans for this place.

"We talked for more than two hours. Raji held my hand across the table the last half hour. He told me all about the Jews in India. There are two main groups. He's from the ones that settled in Mizoram. His ancestors came to India over six hundred years ago…"

"Listen, I can't hear everything now," Natalie interrupted.

Maggie's face fell. "Why not?"

"David will be home in a few minutes and I have to start to organize the packing." *Acceptable white lie*, she told herself. Even her best friend didn't need to know she was about to get ready for some special sex with her husband! "And we can talk tomorrow as we go over to say goodbye to Chaya Sarah."

"Oh, okay. You're right. Let me just tell you one more thing: I slept with him! Now, how can you leave me without the details?"

"Sometimes you just gotta do what you gotta do."

They both laughed and gave each other that sidelong glance that said that's exactly what they each were doing.

"Okay, give me a hug and I'll let you go."

Chapter Eight

Back in her room Natalie put on some make-up, David's favorite perfume, "Love Nest," and for the third time that day took off all her clothes. She lay down naked on the bed and waited for him. Their last night in Jerusalem was going to be something to remember.

David walked in at ten-fifteen. "It's over. I can't believe it. The whole sabbatical…whoa, you're naked! Are you hot? Do you feel sick?"

Natalie replied, "No, I am not sick. And yes, I am hot. But not from the heat. I'm hot because I did something today for us and I kept it a surprise but now I want to share it."

"What in the world did you do?"

"David, do you know what a mikvah is?"

"Sure. My sister went to the mikvah before she got married to her first husband. That was ten years before we got married. They divorced six years later. But he was kind of Conservadox and insisted that she go to the mikvah, at least once. She hated it and never went back. Of course she hated just about everything that went with Lenny, so I never really listened to her remarks anyway.

What does this have to do with us? I never asked you to go, and you never brought it up."

"No, of course not. It didn't exist in my world as a Reform Jew. It was just an old fashioned part of being Jewish that had been left behind in the Old Country."

Natalie was sitting up now, the sheet modestly draped across her chest.

"You looked so sexy lying there naked," David smiled. "You don't have to cover up for me!" David leaned over and kissed her lips. Natalie responded immediately by kissing him back as she pulled him toward her and down onto the bed.

"Hey, let me get out of this shirt and tie! I'll be right back. This mikvah thing sounds like somehow it turned you on. I want to hear more!"

David jumped up and went into the bathroom. Natalie called out to him, "I went to a mikvah tonight as a bride...your bride." Natalie called after him.

"What? I can't hear you." The water was running.

"I went as your bride to the mikvah tonight!" she repeated.

"How the hell did you do that? We've been married for years...twenty-six to be exact. You can't be a bride!"

"Well, Chaya Sarah told me that I could go once as a bride, no matter how long we've been married. I wanted to do it for us, because we're soul mates! Soul mates means we're willing to climb every mountain together. We're there for one another and we get over our disappointments because we have so much love for each other."

"Wait," David interrupted her. "First I need to know more about tonight. Where did you go and how did you get there?" He was so concerned about the details of the evening that he couldn't focus fully on being Natalie's soul mate.

"I don't like you wandering around a city like Jerusalem on your own at night," he continued. "There are dangerous people out there and terrorists. Not everyone is our friend, Natalie! I assume Maggie didn't go with you."

"Of course not! She isn't married anymore, and anyway, who would have wanted to be her ex's soul mate? He was awful. I got the name of the mikvah from Chaya Sarah and I took a taxi both ways. I was perfectly safe." Natalie thought, *I have no idea if I was safe or not. The neighborhood was creepy, the mikvah was awfully quiet, I left the red strings there, and I wrote down our address in the States.*

"I'm so glad we're going home tomorrow night," David sighed. "I don't know who this Chaya Sarah is, but I think she's had enough influence on you."

Natalie felt her temper start to rise, and her passion begin to ebb. "David, here I am feeling all romantic toward you and you're sounding like a punitive father, rather than a sexy husband. And you're making me angry. I haven't followed you around Israel. I don't even know what you did half the time. But I trust you."

"I'm sorry. I love you so much, I just don't want anything to happen to you. I know you think I'm kind of like an absent-minded professor, but you're my life!"

"Oh, David," she said, relieved. "Then you know what I mean about soul mates! We really are each other's soul mate." Loving feelings flowed through Natalie again. The feelings weren't as electrically charged as with Jack, but they made her feel so whole and fully female. Enough to turn on all her juices. She was ready to make love.

David walked by the bed and she let the sheet fall off. She gripped his hand and pulled him toward her. Obviously he was also ready. He lowered himself onto the bed and pulled her toward him. He ran his fingers through her hair and turned her face so they were looking into each others' eyes. They both smiled uncontrollably. She kissed him, and nuzzled her face into his chest, where she could feel the beating of his heart. He lifted her chin and kissed her lips, the little patch of freckles on her nose, her cheeks, her neck, her shoulders, her breasts and more, as he said softly, several times, "my soul mate!"

Chapter Nine

David's responses were heightened, not only from seeing his wife naked and waiting for him, but because of the intensity of their soul mate conversation. Not a man who easily shared his deepest feelings, telling Natalie that she was his life was big.

David moved further down her body with his kisses, and she felt an urge develop "down there" beyond any she'd ever felt before. The urge was so strong; she wanted to push him inside of her *now*. Stronger than when she wanted to get pregnant and knew she was ovulating, even stronger than she'd ever felt toward Jack, the feelings were definitely for David and no one else.

By the time he lovingly kissed the scar lines from her Cesarean births, she was almost over the hill.

"*Now*, David," she whispered.

He understood. It was so good. All of it. And when they finished, Natalie was blissfully worn out.

"I don't want to pack."

"Me neither. Let's just lie here naked until the morning. We have plenty of time tomorrow."

"I love you."

"I love you."

David turned out the light.

"I have to pee." Natalie got up, and on her way back opened the curtains: "Look at the sky! So many stars."

"Mmmm." David was almost asleep. Natalie got back into bed and snuggled next to him. She felt as if she could dissolve into sugar crystals and fairy dust. What a lovely feeling of complete sexual and emotional fulfillment.

Chapter Ten

Apparently Natalie's subconscious mind still was not satisfied. By six in the morning, she moved away from David in the bed so as not to wake him as she tossed and turned. She'd had two unpleasant dreams as dawn approached.

In the first dream she was floating away from David. She tried to hold onto him but she couldn't. She wanted to stand and run toward him but she could only float.

In the second dream she was with Jack. They were discussing how to leave their spouses without creating too much distress. Both David and Jack's wife overheard. David looked broken and said, "you're leaving me aren't you?" Overwhelmed with guilt and shame, Natalie was unable to respond.

She awoke upset, her heart pounding. Why would she dream either dream after such a great night with David? After having made such a clear decision yester-day? Maybe Maggie was right. It wasn't so simple. Jack was misbehaving by pushing himself into her life, but she did really still have feelings for him. Feelings don't lie. They may show up uninvited, but they're very real.

Natalie tossed and turned a while longer but finally fell back to sleep. Fortunately, no alarm had been set, and by the time they both got up at nine o'clock, she felt well rested and back to herself. "Meet you at ten-thirty and we'll head over to say good-bye to Chaya Sarah, okay?" Maggie had called to ask.

"Better make it eleven, I just got up."

"Okay, lobby at eleven. It's gorgeous out. Let's walk over."

"Sure."

At eleven o'clock, Natalie and Maggie met in the lobby. Both women looked radiant. Obviously they had both enjoyed some special moments since they'd last seen each other. Natalie wore a new outfit, a very light weight woolen dress in taupe that was very simple and versatile, and always fell in a way that showed off the touch of a top designer. Maggie also decided to dress up for her last day in Jerusalem and wore a fabulous loose-knit deep maroon sweater over a pale maroon silk blouse. A straight black skirt and a thick black patent leather belt finished the outfit.

"You look great!"

"So do you!"

"Ready?"

"Yes, let's go. We really need to be back by three. The bus for the airport leaves at five-thirty."

"What's David doing?"

"He's looking over his books and papers, discarding the nonessentials, and making some good-bye phone calls. Are you seeing Raji before we leave?"

"He's coming over to see me around three, so I really do have to be back."

"I guess you had a good time?"

"Natalie, do you know what it's like to feel suddenly entranced by someone?"

"Yes, I guess I do." As an aside Natalie thought, *How about being entranced by two people?* She also left unspoken the fact that, right before she came downstairs to the lobby, a text arrived from Jack that had her mind in a new whirl.

His text was simple: *I won't keep writing you. I realize that I put you under tremendous pressure. Have a safe trip. You know where to find me.*

Natalie was aware of a slight let down although she hadn't fully processed the message. It was almost as if he was supposed to pursue her, even though that created unbelievable conflict and pressure.

"Well, I'm entranced by Raji. I need to tell you all about my day yesterday."

"Tell me!" Natalie felt relieved that she could put her own thoughts aside for the long walk.

"First we went to lunch at this great outdoor restaurant. It had a large garden with the most beautiful fruit trees and flowering bushes. We sat under a pear tree. The food was great. Organic and vegetarian. No meat.

"We sat for a long time and talked about how we grew up. So different. And yet there were similarities. He's the youngest of four boys, and two of his brothers still live in India, in Mumbai. They go to the synagogue there and keep kosher. Can you believe that? Between them they have nine children. His other brother is also in England. He's a musician and plays the violin with the London Symphony. He has two children who come and go all the time to Raji's flat.

"Raji loves having the kids visit," Maggie continued. "He's sad that he didn't have children. He was married for ten years to a very bright woman from India whom he actually met in London. She had a big job in a bank and a doctorate in economics. She wasn't Jewish, and he didn't care, but as he thought back, he realized that one of their conflicts was religion. He became much more interested in Judaism and she found that boring.

"After a while it seemed like they didn't agree on anything anymore, even food. He's a vegetarian, she loved her chicken vindaloo, compulsive bridge playing, and her dog. Finally, there just wasn't any reason to stay married."

Maggie stopped long enough to take a breath. "I think like me, but for different reasons, he felt kind of beat up and unappreciated in his marriage. You should have seen how intently he listened to my stories about my marriage. His face was so responsive and caring, and every time I looked into those deep brown eyes I melted a little more. When I told him how my ex is giving a two carat diamond to that bitch secretary he's engaged to, he looked like he was going to cry. No man has ever shown such sincere interest in me before." Now Maggie looked close to tears.

"When we were having dessert, he gently took my hand and caressed it. I was falling apart inside. I knew I was a goner, it was just a matter of time before *it* was going to happen.

"After lunch we started to walk. At first sort of randomly, but eventually we ended up near his apartment in Jerusalem. Did I tell you he has a small apartment here? He actually spends even more time here than Jack. Anyway, he asked me if I wanted to come up to the apartment for a while."

"That sounds pretty direct!" Natalie commented.

"Yes, but you have to understand that we were both so ready for what was going to happen. And we both felt so natural and honest with each other. There was no pressure and no pretense."

"Okay. So then what happened, or shouldn't I ask?"

They both laughed. "Well, we went upstairs to his flat in this lovely modern apartment building right near the Wall. He showed me lots of pictures of his family and pictures of India. We sat on the floor and ate spicy candy that he actually made himself. He loves to cook. It was gooey and covered with sesame seeds and coconut flakes. It was so yummy. Then before I knew it, I was sitting there without my blouse on. We lay down on giant pillows and things happened very fast and then they happened very slowly…"

Maggie looked away, as if she saw every step of their lovemaking again in her head as she talked.

"So, it was wonderful," Natalie responded. "I get that. And you are entranced. But we're going home tonight. You *are* coming home with us?"

"Yes, I'm leaving. Raji and I will write and Skype each other."

"And what about Gary? He'll be waiting for you."

"I'll see. I still like Gary. Let's see how things settle once we're back. I know I can't think straight yet. I'm too over the top for the moment. But even I know there's a part of me that realizes it would be easier in the long run to get involved with Gary. Raji means a complete change of everything. I'm not sure I'm ready to leave Manhattan and live between London and Jerusalem. But we don't have to decide that for today. Today I can just float. And what about you, my dear?"

"Me? I was hoping I could just get you to talk the whole way over," Natalie responded honestly, trying to make it sound more like a joke. "Well, the mikvah was fabulous. I felt so spiritual and close to G-d and close to

David at the same time. It was amazing. And David got a treat when he came home last night. Actually, to be fair, we both got a treat."

"I guess you made wild, passionate love. I assume you didn't order in dessert."

"Yes. It was the best ever. And I felt so much love for David. Like my heart was totally filled with that love."

"You felt it? What does that mean? You don't feel it as much today? Jack is still lurking? Don't hide out on me, miss."

Natalie turned away but Maggie saw her face flush.

"Okay, Natalie. What's going on?"

"Jack wrote to me that he will leave me alone. He respects my situation."

"So, isn't that what you wanted?"

"Yes."

"Then why that deer-in-the-headlights look in your eyes?"

"I feel kind of dumped."

"Would you rather have David dump you? Your soul mate? What are you, crazy?"

"No, G-d forbid! It's complicated. Feelings are different from thoughts."

"Oh, now the psychology stuff. Bottom line is you got stirred up. We both need to get home and out of this fantasy land!"

"I think you're right. At least we'll have one last wonderful chat with Chaya Sarah. Maybe we won't find out all about her, but at least we can take her picture and get her home address and write to her!"

Chapter Eleven

As Natalie and Maggie approached the school for their final "good-byes" with Chaya Sarah, they were shocked to see what appeared to be a totally closed-up building. "Look, the windows are all closed and it's pretty warm out now," Natalie observed.

"I don't hear the children's lovely voices. I wonder why it's so quiet." Maggie frowned.

"I don't see any cars parked in the parking lot."

"None of the girls are on the playground."

The closer they got to the school, the more abandoned it appeared.

"I think the front door has a chain lock on it!"

"That's weird." Now it was Natalie's turn to frown. "Let's check in the back. Maybe something happened with the school, but Chaya Sarah is still in her office."

"That doesn't make sense," Maggie argued. "She works for the school."

"We don't really know that. We just assumed that."

"Okay, let's check."

Natalie felt her heart pounding as they walked around to the back of the school.

"I'm really scared," Maggie said. "It's too damned quiet. It doesn't make any sense."

The door looked the same as every other time they'd visited.

"You knock," Maggie challenged her friend.

"No, you knock."

"No, you knock. You're the brave one."

"Okay, let's both knock."

Their knock was answered only by dead silence. No radiant woman opened the door. No smile greeted them. No Chaya Sarah to usher them into the cozy simple office and offer them tea and cream cookies.

"This is horrible." Natalie lamented.

Maggie began to cry. "I can't believe she just isn't here. Maybe she left us a note. How can we leave Israel and not see her? It's like she never existed!"

Natalie handed Maggie a tissue. "Come on. We can't just stand here crying. Let's find out what happened to the school."

"Okay, but first let's look around for a note."

The two women scoured the bushes near the door, looked in the dirt, and investigated the window sills for whatever they could find. Satisfied that there was nothing to find but some gum wrappers and a page from a child's notebook, they finally went back to the street.

"Look, there's a mother!" Natalie cried, "Maybe she'll know what happened."

A woman approached pushing two babies in a carriage. Three more children of various ages walked behind her like scattered ducklings, as the mother came closer and closer.

"Excuse us," Natalie addressed her, "we're trying to find out why this school is closed."

The woman looked bewildered. Obviously she didn't speak English. She looked away from them quickly and pushed ahead with her carriage and little charges.

"Here comes a man," Maggie noticed. "Let's ask him."

A man in Hassidic garb walked toward them, hand-in-hand with a boy of about eight.

"Sir, can you help us?" Natalie tried again. "We want to know what happened to this school?"

The man spoke some English. "School? No good, that school."

"What do you mean?" Maggie asked.

"No good. Not for you. Come, Yosef."

It was clear he was moving on and no more information would be forthcoming.

"What was that all about?" Maggie wondered aloud.

"I don't know, but it didn't sound good," Natalie responded. "Let's start back to the hotel."

Chapter Twelve

Maggie wanted to stay. "How can we leave? What if something bad happened?"

"Look, it's terrible that Chaya Sarah isn't here and it's a mystery why the school is closed, but we have to get on with our day. As we walk we can ask more people about the school."

They stopped people as best they could for the first few blocks but many didn't speak English. Several people avoided them, perhaps because they were clearly not from a religious neighborhood. Men in particular were not eager to speak to the women. However, one man was quite chatty. Unfortunately, his English left much to be desired. He explained animatedly that the school had been in financial difficulty, that the teachers were not paid on time and more recently not at all, and that in his opinion the school had to close. He had expected it for months. Pretty soon it would be for sale, he concluded.

"This is terrible news," Maggie said as they walked on. "Maybe that is why Chaya Sarah always looked so distressed when she would get those strange phone calls? Maybe she was trying to raise money for the school?"

"Maybe it was worse than that. Maybe someone in the school was stealing money. That happened in the United States. I remember reading about a private school in the States where money laundering took place."

"Do you know what money laundering is?"

"No, but I know it's illegal!"

"I think we should stop in and report the school to the police."

"What, tell them a big school building is locked and we think that is strange and they should check it? They would think we're crazy."

"And to think we don't even know Chaya Sarah's last name!"

"And now she will never know about my night at the mikvah," Natalie sighed." I was just there yesterday. This is so unbelievable."

Maggie shed a tear every once in a while, while Natalie felt a kind of angry frustration that she couldn't pinpoint at the moment, but that she recognized well. It was an unpleasant and harsh feeling that made her feel like she could explode inside.

Meanwhile, deeply engrossed in their conversation as they walked to and from the school, they missed a number of events occurring around them.

They missed the proclamations of the local newspaper headlines: *Police Suspect Latest Terrorist Plots Involve Additional Infiltrators!* as they walked by a newsstand.

The streets contained much more trash than usual waiting for pick-up, as people scrubbed their homes for Passover.

They didn't notice the small section of the women's side of the Wall that had been roped off as policewomen searched all females who entered the open portion.

Nor did they see the children's clothing store, filled to the brim with mothers, carriages, toddlers and older children, all eager to buy new clothes for the holiday.

In addition, a young woman had slipped unnoticed inside the back entrance of a boarded-up small brick building that once had been a mikvah years ago.

Natalie and Maggie were also oblivious to the wailing of police and ambulance sirens in the distance.

As they neared the hotel, discouraged and drained, they encountered a group of young, exuberant Americans, laughing and talking as they walked together to the Wall for the first time. They were part of Birthright, a free ten-day trip to Israel sponsored by a Jewish philanthropist and offered to any young adult with Jewish roots. Even this wasn't enough to lift their spirits.

Chapter Thirteen

Back at the hotel, Natalie called David and asked him to come down and join them for lunch at the restaurant next door before they did the final packing.

The sunshine felt good as they basked in the early afternoon warmth on the restaurant's terrace. Lemon sole with avocado and ripe olives, along with delicious small onion rolls, helped a little to calm the women down.

David immediately recognized the signs of distress. Natalie had that sharp look in her eyes he remembered seeing on her grandmother's face when they were first married. It always meant that trouble was brewing or Natalie's grandmother and grandfather were at each other again. It used to seem funny to David that a couple so elderly could cat fight. But still, he never liked conflict, so he didn't like that look in either grandma's or his wife's eyes.

"What's wrong?" David asked.

Maggie jumped in with the story before Natalie could tame it down a bit. She already knew how much David was bound to criticize their adventure. Disturbed enough by it already, even the romance last night wouldn't make up for David's concerns about his wife getting close to a stranger.

Sure enough, David's reaction was quick and sharp as soon as Maggie described the locked school building and the remarks by the stranger. He realized that it was a school in distress, with maybe some illegal stuff happening inside.

"What the hell were both of you doing anyway?" David admonished them both. "I knew there was trouble brewing! Great, now it turns out that maybe the whole school is involved in something illegal. Maybe it's even a front for terrorists."

"That's ridiculous!" Natalie practically shouted back. But inside, she wasn't so sure. *What if it wasn't kosher?* she mused. *Don't innocent people like herself and Maggie get duped all the time?*

But at the same time, *getting to know Chaya Sarah was amazing!* another part of her told herself. *The adventures I had were unbelievable. She made me feel great and I learned so much!*

"So, once again," David was saying, "tell me everything that Chaya Sarah knows about us. Is it just our names, where we live and our phone numbers? Or is it our bank accounts also?" The sarcasm in David's voice was thick.

Even Maggie cringed a little inside. "She doesn't know my bank information," she answered David. "Natalie, didn't you make out a check for a donation to the school? I gave cash."

Natalie shot a death glance at Maggie. "Thanks for remembering. But anyway, what difference does that make? Everyone who has a checking account has numbers on it."

"And does she have your e-mail address?" David asked.

"No, we never talked about e-mail."

"Isn't it on your business card, Natalie? Maggie once again piped up. "You gave it to her when you wanted her to know how to reach us in case there were changes to the plans about the Purim party." As an afterthought, Maggie added in a very soft, pensive voice, "that she never came to."

"Well, at least when we get home you can change your e-mail account."

I don't want to, Natalie thought, *I don't want to! What if Chaya Sarah tries to reach us?*

Out loud she mumbled, "I guess so."

"Not to worry," Maggie suddenly brightened up. "When we get back I'll fill Gary in on everything. He knows a lot already, because I e-mail him all the time. He can find out stuff for us. He's a detective. I bet he can get in touch with the police here and answer all our questions."

Suddenly the atmosphere lightened. David seemed content for the moment with the idea that a fellow American could do some sleuthing beyond the capacities of his wife and her best friend.

Maggie was happy she'd figured out how they could find the truth, and in her mind was thinking if there was anything bad discovered then maybe they would also be able to figure out how to help Chaya Sarah. Raji slipped into the back of her mind for the moment. But of course, as in all things complicated, he would only stay in the back of her mind for a little while.

Natalie was still agitated, now angry at her husband for putting down an adventure that had been so important to her. She couldn't see for the moment that he was coming from a position of protecting her. She could only feel how diminished he made her feel. She kept looking at her phone and realized she was also disappointed that there were no texts. Jack was keeping his word and leaving her alone. This was not a good day. At least not so far.

Just then David's cell rang. He stepped away as Natalie and Maggie finished their coffee. "Sounds great, let me check with the ladies," he said as he walked back to the table, cell in hand.

"Dr. Simon and his wife Althea want to take us on a quick ride around Jerusalem, just one last look and then out for supper and on to the airport. He said we'll have plenty of time since our takeoff has been delayed until eleven-thirty. I'll cancel our cab. I think it would be a lot of fun. His wife used to be a tour guide in the city, so it'll also be very informative."

Natalie and Maggie both nodded their heads in agreement. Both were relieved to have a distraction that would bring them up to the end of their stay in Jerusalem.

David turned his attention back to his phone.

"Great! We'll be ready for you and Althea at five. Thanks."

"Remember Dr. Simon did a lot to help me arrange my sabbatical here?" he asked Natalie.

"I remember you were writing to him before we left Norwalk."

The atmosphere continued to lighten, and soon Maggie was back in her room and they were all busy packing. Natalie took a shower and rested a while with her cell at her side. Still there were no texts.

• • •

Maggie sent an e-mail to Gary with more details of their adventure today and also chatted on the phone at length with Raji.

David wrote in his journal while Natalie rested. He always kept a detailed account of all his talks, meetings, impressions, and psychological insights. But although his thoughts ended up on paper, Natalie's stayed in her head.

Chapter Fourteen

Five o'clock came soon enough. The Simons pulled up on the dot as their passengers stood under the hotel canopy, luggage packed and ready to go.

A very distinguished looking guy in his early sixties, Dr. Joel Simon sported a full head of totally white hair that made him look handsomely mature. His steel blue eyes were penetrating, yet friendly. He probably made an excellent psychiatrist. Althea's energy proved to be abundant, and her mass of gray curls, graceful slim body and pretty face with soft brown eyes and beautiful clear skin seemed a living example of how wonderful aging can be.

What a whirlwind ride! Althea must have been the most amazing city guide, as she seemed to know everything. First, she suggested a quick visit to the Wall. She happily shared miracle stories of prayers being answered after people prayed at the Wall, as they drove over and parked.

Her favorite was about an American man who prayed at the Wall for the chance to reconnect with his son after he'd gone off in a huff at age twenty-five. Three years had passed, and the father deeply regretted some of his remarks. The son, then working in France, refused all contact with his family. The man prayed and, as he walked slowly back to his hotel, who do you think walked right by him? His son! The man called out his name, and "the rest was history," according to Althea. Startled, the son turned around, and when he recognized his father, started to weep. They embraced, and from that moment on, they not only reconciled, but the son returned to the United States to work in the family business.

As they approached the Wall, the two men headed for the men's side. On the women's side, Natalie touched the wall, closed her eyes, and prayed for peace of mind and a safe journey home. It was so easy now to get into an intense short prayer. She actually felt tears form as the emotions inside sought some kind of relief. Maggie's eyes remained open; it was too hard to pray right now as she thought about never seeing Raji again. She also wondered what had happened at the locked-up school, and thought about how miserable she hoped her ex's secretary would be once she was married to him!

The women found themselves once again accosted by the gypsy-like women with red strings as they left the Wall. Natalie and Maggie found themselves somehow with three red strings attached to their wrists by the time they returned to the car, "for good luck."

Althea already wore a red string on her wrist. "We live in a very complex culture here," she explained. "A lot of unexplainable and mystical things happen in Jerusalem. It's a city alive with history and spiritual energy and it doesn't hurt to wear a little protection!" She showed Natalie and Maggie the sterling silver "hand of G-d" embedded with semi-precious stones that she wore around her neck. "Joel gave it to me on our tenth anniversary. I never take it off."

"What do you mean unexplainable and mystical things?" asked Natalie.

"There are definitely amazing energies here," Althea chatted, back in the car. "It's similar to a vortex, like they talk about in Sedona. Maybe it's because so many people from such varied backgrounds have come here for thousands of years to pray. Who knows? Some people say it's because the universe came into being at the very spot right behind the Wall. Again, who knows? We only know that people feel and behave differently here. Sometimes it's wonderful, but sometimes it's too much for people to handle. We have something called the Jerusalem Syndrome."

"What's that?" Natalie asked.

"Don't you remember?" Maggie chimed in, "I mentioned that to you when you first arrived here. I heard about it years ago."

"That's when people are so overcome by their spiritual experiences here that they think they're Jesus Christ, or Mother Mary, or Moses," Althea explained.

"Wow, that's amazing! What happens to those people?"

"Sometimes it wears off, but sometimes they have to be hospitalized. Other times they need to leave. Not everyone snaps out of it, and that can be very sad. We have experts who work with people who exhibit evidence of the syndrome."

"That's scary stuff," said Natalie. "I feel bad for them."

"Joel has given many papers on the subject. That is one of his niches in psychiatry."

"Let's talk about the more pleasant aspects of living in Jerusalem," Joel said, changing the subject. "One of the nicest is eating. The food is wonderful here — it's fresh and you can find any food from around the world because of the diverse groups that live here. By the way, I have a special surprise for you for supper tonight."

"What is it?" David asked.

"Just wait and see! It's a bit of a drive. Another twenty minutes of touring and we'll be there."

"No hints?"

"No, but you'll always remember it. I promise."

Althea continued their guided tour over the next twenty minutes. She seemed to know everything about everywhere! They drove past many of the main buildings in Jerusalem, including the Yad Vashem Holocaust Museum, Israel's Parliament called the Knesset, and the Prime Minister's residence.

Eventually they left the major downtown area and appeared to be driving through residential neighborhoods. Some of the streets they passed looked like those near the mikvah, Natalie thought. She wondered vaguely why they would be passing through that part of town.

"We're almost there," Joel told them. "I guess it's time to let you in on my little surprise. We're going to a special restaurant in East Jerusalem that has the best Middle Eastern food in the city. Most tourists don't get to come here, though it's perfectly safe, just off of the tourist radar."

Natalie suddenly felt her heart pounding. *Oh, my G-d,* she thought. *Could it be where Jack and Raji took us?*

Maggie looked a bit distraught, but neither woman dared to say a word.

"Just down this block, the Adelphia Restaurant, known to locals for its great food and belly dancers. I'm sure you'll get a big kick out of it!"

Natalie felt like throwing up. Maggie almost choked on the water she'd been sipping. What if the maître d' or the waiters remember us? Everyone that night seemed to know Jack and Raji!

Natalie held onto her red strings for dear life. Maggie prayed, *please G-d let this not be a nightmare!*

Chapter Fifteen

David was smiling, unaware of the women's reactions. "I can't wait to try the food. Will we get to see the belly dancing?"

Natalie noticed three limousines as they got out of the car. What if one of them had brought Jack and Raji? They said they came here a lot.

Natalie had forgotten how chilly one could feel even when it was warm out. She imagined this to be the kind of chill they talked about in old romance novels when the heroine walked into a room where a ghost was lurking. Maybe soon she'd feel the cold draft that those rooms always seemed to contain.

Dr. Simon led the way and chatted with the maître d'. Obviously he was well known here, just like Jack and Ragi. Soon, with a great deal of pomp and circumstance, they were escorted by the maître d' to a front row table.

Apparently they would be there just long enough to see one short belly dance. David smiled from ear to ear. Natalie hadn't realized how much he enjoyed such things! Once, when they were young, they'd visited a restaurant with a belly dancer. She had forgotten how turned-on David had become and how she'd tried to move her hips the same way as the dancer when they got home. She hadn't succeeded and they'd both started laughing. Soon they were on the bed, drinking wine and making love. It turned out pretty good anyway.

Wow, that was a long buried memory, Natalie thought as the maître d' pulled out her low chair and assisted her to sit. She tried not to look directly at him, but too late. He was one of those guys who never forgot a face.

"Delighted to see you back here, madam," he said. Natalie stood frozen with panic until she realized that the noise level in the restaurant was quite high. The ceiling there contained no special noise-absorbing tiles and the place was already full, even this early. It would have been impossible for anyone except herself to hear him. She relaxed, smiled, and sat down.

Apparently Maggie received the same greeting, as evidenced by the expression in her eyes when she looked at Natalie after she was seated.

The two women now became secret telepathic co-horts, praying that nothing else would happen. Maybe the irony of being brought to the same restaurant where they had been escorted by two men, presumed to be their dates by the outside world, would be funny in a few weeks or months, but not now. Now all they could do was try to make small talk and glance furtively at the front door.

There was one other scary moment. It was when the same limo driver who had driven them and was supposed to be Jack's bodyguard appeared and stood near the front entrance. What in the world was he doing here?

Did he bring Jack and, in my attempt not to be recognized, I didn't notice? Natalie wondered. *Is he following me?* Now seriously afraid to look around, she thought, *maybe Jack stopped texting me but he's not leaving me alone! Maybe he's having me followed. Oh, my G-d. I'm having insane thoughts. We can't get on the plane too soon!*

Maggie must have wondered also, as the fellow stood, looking stern and very much like a muscled bodyguard. However, he never acknowledged them, and about twenty minutes before they left, he disappeared with no Jack in sight, just as the belly dancer came onto the small stage.

David was definitely mesmerized. He never took his eyes off the woman who, thank G-d, was not the same performer as the previous evening. She moved beautifully and her satin brown hair came down below her waist, swirling as she gyrated. David eagerly held Natalie's hand across the table, obviously smitten with both the belly dancer and his wife.

Natalie and Maggie made a quick trip to the bathroom before they left. "I can't believe any of this!" Maggie groaned.

"I can't either."

"What was Jack's driver and bodyguard doing here?"

"Maybe he was following me?"

"Yeah, I was thinking the same thing."

Natalie's face fell. "I was just kidding, having crazy thoughts."

"Well, it *is* strange."

Just then Althea Simon entered the restroom, putting an end to their chat.

"We love this place," she smiled. It's just about our favorite restaurant. A few years ago there was a shooting here, but since then all has been quiet. Some guy came here to hunt down his wife, who'd been cheating on him. Kind of bizarre, like a movie plot."

"Was she killed?"

"Yes, along with the boyfriend and his friends. It wasn't pretty."

Natalie and Maggie each responded with their best false smiles. *My life is a little like a movie plot right now,* Natalie thought.

Curious, Maggie wanted more details. " Well, the man who started the restaurant is half Jewish and half Muslim," Althea reported. "He put his money and even his life on the line to start this restaurant on the edge of East Jerusalem. This is one of the only neighborhoods where both Jewish and Muslim families live side by side, all Israeli citizens. The restaurant gained quite a following and actually none of the political conflicts have played out here. Only an irate husband with a cheating wife who went berserk here."

Soon they were back in the car and on their way to the airport. They couldn't arrive soon enough for Natalie, who didn't particularly enjoy hearing about a love triangle that ended in murder. Not that David was capable of that kind of thing…but still …

"Don't be strangers," Dr. Simon was saying. "Please come back again. All of you can always stay with us. We have two spare bedrooms now that the kids are grown. We'll take you to more off-the–beaten-path places. I promise."

Great! Natalie thought sarcastically.

Chapter Sixteen

At 12:02 a.m. their flight took off on time and they were homeward bound. Sleepy, but stirred up, Natalie tortured herself about whether to take a Xanax. Maybe she didn't really need it. On the other hand, maybe she did. She finally decided not to take one unless she found herself still awake in an hour or two.

Her dilemma stemmed from the fact that a text had appeared just as she'd pushed the button to turn off her cell phone. She'd been able only to read part of it, *will miss you, sorry,* before her phone shut off.

As she leaned back and tried to relax, her mind went into a tailspin. *I guess Jack decided to resurface and pull at my heartstrings again. But why do I assume it was Jack? He gave his word that he'd leave me alone. But is his word any good?*

Her mind whirled with other possibilities. *Maybe it was Chaya Sarah finally checking in,* she thought. *Maybe Maggie got the same message. Did Chaya Sarah even know how to text? She didn't seem the type, but looks can be deceiving. Maybe it wasn't either of them.*

Maybe it was Althea Simon just being nice. But why would she say she was sorry?

David held her hand and started to doze as the conversation in her mind continued in circles. She noticed Maggie writing busily on her iPad, probably filling Gary in with the latest so that he could be ready to do some detective work around the locked school and Chaya Sarah.

Natalie found herself in a half dream state. She heard all that was going on around her, the muffled roar of the plane's engines, the chatter of people not yet ready to sleep, the flight attendants beginning their first round of drinks and snacks. But at the same time she experienced short dreams, so real for a few seconds: Chaya Sarah taking off her modest long-sleeved blouse and long skirt, and revealing underneath a short red skirt and a bolero top with very short sleeves; Jack standing next to her with his arm around her; Jack pulling her to him; people running screaming down a street. The last one jarred her fully awake.

The flight attendant appeared and Natalie requested two glasses of seltzer with no ice.

Clearly, she was not about to fall asleep. She decided to skip the unpleasant dreams for a while. She looked at David sleeping so peacefully, his mouth slightly open, his hand now resting in a familiar way on her thigh. He was handsome for his age, she thought. His hair was still dark brown and wavy. His features were good, and he had a strong chin.

She remembered her mother mentioning his strong features when they were dating. She had also told Natalie that if she wanted to know how he would age, to look at his parents. She had. At the time they were in their early fifties, just about David's age now. They were nice looking; his dad was only slightly balding and not at all gray. His mother had a very pretty face with bright sparkling eyes. Natalie had been satisfied and of course, what did it matter? She was in love.

As it turned out, David fared even better physically than his parents. Twice-a-week workouts at the local Jewish Center and a once-a-week tennis foursome kept him in excellent shape.

She scrutinized his face, noticed the shape of his nose and mouth. He was so much a part of her that it was hard to see him as a separate person. It was almost like looking at herself. His hand was so familiar, almost an extension of her being. And yet, as she looked at him she couldn't feel the electricity she had felt with Jack. Instead, she felt comfort and ease. She wouldn't call it exciting any more than she'd call her left arm exciting. She was thankful that it was still there doing all of its chores every day, but it was just her left arm.

Why was that? Why was it so easy to feel tingling and arousal when she thought of Jack? There was such a magical allure in the resurgence of such powerful feelings. It was almost like they were both giant magnets positioned at the precise point where the pull of attraction is the greatest. At that moment everything feels okay.

She thought, *what if I could have both of them? Did women ever have more than one husband? What if both could make love to me at the same time? Jack could lie on the right side of me and David on the left. I would be out of my mind with arousal. No, I've got to get Jack out of my mind! I thought I'd really succeeded last night, and now I'm imagining a threesome! This has got to stop. All these feelings are just an illusion of what I think we would still have. Jack was a jerk emotionally and he probably still is.*

Natalie decided to watch a movie. One of her favorites was playing, "Midnight in Paris." She loved the parts when the main character walks away from his life and finds himself in Paris in the 1920's. It was so charmingly done and you never actually know if he's found an entrance to a time dimension or whether he's imagining the whole thing or maybe hallucinating. And it never even matters. The story just flows.

As she watched Owen Wilson walk into the 1920's one more time, Natalie thought to herself, *I wonder if something like that happened to us with Chaya Sarah? How do we know that she was real? How do we know that we didn't walk in and out of some other dimension that we don't know about? Maybe she just materialized when it was time for us to learn something? Maybe we'll find out that there's really an apartment house right where we thought there was a school?*

Meanwhile, to the right of Natalie, Maggie was writing a detailed e-mail to Gary that she'd send as soon as they landed. *So you must get ready to help us see what happened to Chaya Sarah I'm so glad you're a detective. We really need your expertise!*

The problem is that I think somehow she's in trouble. Something doesn't feel right to me. And I've got very good instincts. I knew my son had appendicitis months before the doctor recognized the signs. I knew when my mother was sick even before she did. It's not so great to have instincts this on-target. But I do. So something is wrong.

I had one idea, Gary. I read about a woman who didn't know she was Jewish until she was thirty and her mom was dying. She'd actually grown up thinking she was a Muslim. She heard her mom, extremely ill, say "Shema Israel..." in her bed. You know we're supposed to say the Shema, not only two times a day, but before we die. So this woman asked her mom, "why are you saying that Jewish prayer?" And very faintly her mom answered, "because I'm Jewish. I never told you." And then she died. So I'm thinking that maybe something like that happened to Chaya Sarah. Maybe she found out she was Jewish and escaped from an Arab home somewhere. She became very learned in Judaism but she's kind of in hiding from people who are furious that she identifies now as a Jew. Maybe some of the people she's running from are terrorists. Maybe they want her to teach them how to appear like religious Jews so they can go into malls and buses with hidden bombs.

What do you think? Anyway, something is off and we need to help her. I have other ideas. I'll tell you more when I see you. Are you taking me out to dinner when I get back? I'll have jet lag but I can't wait to see you...

Completely absorbed now in the movie, Natalie watched the part where the one young lady goes further back in time to live in the days of the Moulin Rouge. She never comes back to the 1920's. *Did her friends and relatives spend the rest of their lives looking for her?* Natalie wondered. *Kind of cruel of her to just leave. Like Chaya Sarah leaving us stranded. Like Batyag never returning after she invited us to her wedding. Just never coming back. It's cruel to leave people in the dark.*

I could never leave David, but it's going to be hard to go home and settle in. I've been somewhere else on too many levels to just go back to Stamford and give intelligence tests to third graders. G-d, I hope I don't get depressed. Good thing Passover's in a couple of days. It'll give me something to get ready for, and it'll be fun to be with our friends and relatives for the Passover Seders. I hope our life gets back to normal. I hope Jack stays in touch once in a while. No, I hope I never hear from him again. I'm tired.

Finally, sleep sneaked up on Natalie.

Meanwhile Maggie was writing another note, this time to Raji and this time with pen and paper, hoping the personal touch would keep her in his mind. *"I miss you already. It was such a special couple of days with you. I don't know what to think at this point. I'm going back to my world and you are in yours. I guess we have to see what happens. I'm thinking about being with you. It was really special. Don't forget me ..."*

Chapter Seventeen

They landed, and as soon as the cell phones could be turned on Natalie searched for the message, and there it was: *"Will miss you, sorry..."* It was from Raji. The rest of the text said simply that he was sorry he couldn't get to the airport to say goodbye to both Natalie and Maggie and to meet David. He hoped they would return sometime soon. Not a peep from Jack. Natalie was relieved and distressed at the same time. As a psychologist she gave herself credit for being able to have two opposite emotions simultaneously and still stay sane. As a woman she hated to be in this predicament.

Maggie turned to Natalie. "Wasn't it nice that Raji wrote to you also. He's such a dear!"

Maggie is so comfortable with everything, Natalie thought as they hugged and went their separate ways. *Here we are best friends, both dealing with two men in our lives, and I'm miserable and Maggie is so happy. She doesn't feel any guilt dangling two different men. Of course, I'm married and she isn't. She had a rotten marriage. But I have a good marriage, so why all these mixed-up feelings?*

The rest of Natalie's day was a jet-lag blur. She was suddenly faced with a house that had been closed for a month, a laundry basket full of mail, some half-dying plants (even though neighbors had checked the house and watered them), some rotten food in the refrigerator, messages on the house phone that had sat for weeks, and a bad smell coming from a corner of the great room; was there a leak seeping into the area carpet that was near the sliding glass door? The challenges seemed to go on and on.

David almost immediately set off to the college to check his mail and messages.

After phone calls to her parents, kids and a couple of close friends, and a tuna fish sandwich (where was that lovely waitress who served them on the beautiful terrace overlooking Jerusalem?), Natalie fell into bed, exhausted and dragging. She forced herself to watch a couple of TV shows but by nine-thirty she fell sound asleep. She never heard David come in.

The rest of the day was also a blur for Maggie, but it ended happily with a lovely dinner. Gary took her out to her favorite restaurant on West 72nd Street. Delighted to be back in her neighborhood, she showered and dressed for her date, and put on one of her new dresses from Jerusalem.

Gary's eyes grew wide and he let out a soft whistle when he saw her. Obviously he was still smitten. All the adventuring in Jerusalem must have coursed through her veins and augmented her glow. Her auburn curls shining from a quick shampoo, her face flushed and glowing and her A-plus figure for a woman close to fifty all came together for a smashing re-entry into her world.

Gary gathered Maggie in his arms for a deep kiss. Maggie responded; however she was definitely in control of the situation, and soon they were out the door of her apartment and walking to Alfredo's.

"Well, what do you think about Chaya Sarah?" Maggie asked as soon as they ordered their large fresh salads and vegetarian pizza made with whole wheat flour. "What about my idea that she may be involved with terrorists but not because she wants to be?"

Gary looked like he was searching to find the right words and trying not to be discouraging. "Your story-line about Chaya Sarah was very interesting and stuff for a good novel, but really, it's based on nothing. You have absolutely no evidence that she's in trouble or that she grew up not knowing she was Jewish."

Maggie's face fell. "I suppose you're right. But I just know in my gut that she's in trouble."

"What can I do as a detective in White Plains?"

"Can't you get the police in Jerusalem to look into the situation?"

"Okay, let's say I can find an officer or detective there willing to try for me. What should I tell him?"

"Tell them about the school. I have the address. How it was suddenly shut down and tell them…well, I don't exactly know. See if they have any information on Chaya Sarah."

"Do you know her last name or phone number?"

"No."

"Well, you're not making this easy, but all right, I'll try to make a contact within the Jerusalem police force. But don't expect much."

"Oh, Gary, you're a dear. Thank you!"

"Meanwhile, what does Chaya Sarah know about you?"

"Well, I gave her one of my business cards. It has my home address on it, since I work out of the apartment, and my cell phone number. That's about it. Oh, and my e-mail address."

"Maybe she'll get in touch with you!"

"Maybe. I just worry that she might not be able to. I have this feeling that I'm supposed to protect her. I don't know why. She's just so unusual, it's almost like she was an angel. She made us both feel so special and attended to."

"Don't I do that?" Gary asked with a chuckle.

"This was different," Maggie explained seriously. "Like all our ideas and emotions and feelings were so important and valuable. Any words that we spoke were worth concentrating on one hundred percent, and any feelings we had were precious. I haven't felt that way since I was a little girl sitting on my grandmother's lap on her front porch, as she laughed, clapped my hands together, sang to me, and kissed my face with an exuberance that made me feel so totally loved!

"And Chaya Sarah was the first person in years who could answer any of my questions about Judaism in a way that made me excited to be Jewish. She made me feel like being Jewish is a most extraordinary journey that I have unwittingly put on hold for so many years, but that I don't have to anymore."

"Then you might be interested in the talk I'm going to tomorrow night at the Jewish Community Center. It's on Passover themes, and exploring our journey from bondage to freedom."

"That sounds great," Maggie responded immediately. *I wish I could talk about Passover with Chaya Sarah!* she thought.

"Maybe I can reach someone in Jerusalem before I see you tomorrow night." Gary took Maggie's hand and pulled her toward him affectionately as they strolled back to her apartment building. It was clear he was hoping for more than a good night kiss.

Later at the door to her apartment, Maggie gently pushed Gary away after a lingering kiss. "I'm too tired for more. Maybe tomorrow night."

Chapter Eighteen

Maggie woke up on her first full day back in the United States happy and full of energy. She loved everything about her day: buying her favorite latte drink at the local Starbuck's, opening all her mail, getting her nails done, doing laundry, letting clients know via e-mail that she was back in town. She chatted happily about her daily life with Raji by e-mail, and read about his diamond business deals and his fondness for her. She also looked forward eagerly to attending the lecture with Gary that night. Maybe he already had information about Chaya Sarah! She was not caught between two men. Rather, she comfortably positioned herself in two different worlds, each with a different man in it.

Miles away, Natalie felt miserable after waking up with a headache. Fortunately, she wasn't due back at school until the week after next, since school vacation started today and ran through next week. This was one of those years when the Easter holidays coincided with Passover, so everyone had a nice long break.

Obviously David had slept in the bed, as his pajamas were on the floor, but he was already gone when she got up.

She dragged around the house for several hours, finally got to the supermarket and completed a number of other small chores, but she couldn't fully lift her mood. Norwalk was a letdown after Jerusalem. She missed everything, the hotel, the busy streets, the amazing mix of cultures, the sharpened energy that had surrounded her, the delicious foods, all their adventures. And of course she missed Chaya Sarah.

Although she didn't want to admit it, she also missed Jack. His closeness had aroused her and brought back the young woman who still lived inside. She had passions that had been forgotten, and with Jack nearby, they'd been triggered again. Her body missed the electricity.

But she now began to realize that Chaya Sarah had introduced her to a different part of herself. It was an ageless, potentially wise and certainly needy part of her that wanted to share one hundred percent in the romance of being alive. It was the part that still needed to nurse at the metaphorical breast of a woman who could teach her what she needed to know to grow old with grace, good humor and little fear. It was the part of herself that had just begun to develop the courage to peek out from behind all the other parts of herself. And that part couldn't survive and flourish on its own yet.

She hadn't even known she had that part until Chaya Sarah made her aware of dimensions of thinking about herself and her marriage and her traditions to which she had never before been exposed. Despite Natalie's anger at the fact that Chaya Sarah hadn't shown up when she was supposed to, she appreciated the fact that this woman had led her to experiences beyond her imagination. She never knew how people celebrated a simcha, the sense of joy that was permitted and encouraged. She never knew that emotions around her marriage could be experienced at such an intimate level of the soul. Now she knew there was a lot more to learn but she no longer had any guidance.

Her cell rang and it was Maggie inviting Natalie and David into the city to join her for the lecture. "You have to come into town. Gary is going to try to get some information today from the Israeli police about Chaya Sarah and the school!"

"How can he? We don't even know her last name."

"I gave him the name and address of the school. I bet he can find out a lot. Please come! The lecture is at seven p.m. for just an hour and then we can all go out for coffee."

"I don't know, I've been so tired and had an awful headache earlier today."

"But you have tomorrow off and all next week! And so does David. Where is that spirited adventurous woman I just spent time with in Israel?"

"I don't know. I've been looking for her all day."

They both laughed. "I'll check with David and get back to you later."

Chapter Nineteen

The lecture was at the West Side Jewish Center. David agreed to the night out, since the Community College was already on spring break and he had taken care of his most pressing messages and correspondence.

Natalie managed to pull herself together. A couple of Tylenol lifted her headache, and a swim at the Norwalk Jewish Center removed some of the stiffness and fatigue from her body. They hadn't met Gary yet and both were curious about this new guy in Maggie's life. It would be fun to meet him.

Natalie was of course intrigued with the calm manner in which Maggie handled having two love interests at the same time. As she got ready for the one-hour drive into Manhattan, Natalie felt better and better. Soon she was singing some of her favorite tunes as she took a quick shower and did her make-up. *I don't look so bad for a jet-lagged middle-aged woman who loves her husband, misses her old boyfriend (even though it's crazy) and is busy wondering if she imagined an Israeli woman named Chaya Sarah. But then again, was she even Israeli?*

"Let's go or we'll be late," David called from the other end of the house.

As they entered the Jewish Center, they saw Maggie standing across the lobby talking to a nice looking guy. Natalie felt that lovely rush of affection for Maggie that one feels for a best friend.

Maggie introduced them to Gary, who looked like one of those older men whose physique had benefited from twenty or thirty years of bicycling and race walking. He exuded energy, and his hazel eyes were kind. Natalie immediately saw why Maggie would feel very comfortable with him. He wasn't exotic like Raji. He was one hundred percent Jewish American. He was comforting, not thrilling. *Isn't that what David is?* Natalie thought. *Enough!*

After the initial introductions and casual conversation, they moved up to the fifth floor for the Passover lecture. Gary mentioned on the way up that he had some initial information about their school, but though the ladies begged him to tell, he wouldn't. "Afterwards," he said, "when we get to the diner I'll share. It's not a lot, but it's a start. I got hold of a young detective on the Jerusalem police force who agreed to do some research, and within a few hours he called back."

Natalie and Maggie were intrigued. "Just a tidbit?" Maggie begged.

"Well the school does exist," He revealed. "You didn't imagine it. Later I'll get out my notes."

The classroom filled quickly for the lecture, mostly people fifty years and up.

David, himself a lecturer, commented, "I'm really interested in seeing what Deborah Stone has to say, she's very respected as a Jewish scholar who often speaks on the hidden and less apparent meanings of our rituals.

"It's when we reach fifty and older that we begin to think more profoundly about things like religious holidays. We want to know why we are doing all sorts of rituals that we've done forever. Sometimes we realize that we don't really know the meaning behind them, or the history."

"I didn't realize the lecturer tonight is a woman! Natalie exclaimed.

"So what?" Maggie prodded.

"So nothing. Let me see her write-up."

Dr. Deborah Stone had apparently earned many credentials, including a doctorate in Jewish studies from Brandeis University, a master's degree in social psychology from Yale, and a full professorship at Yeshiva University. She lived for many years in Israel and authored a book titled *Coming Home to Universal Messages in the Torah.*

Tiny, exuberant, and in her late forties, Dr. Stone spoke passionately, and Natalie and Maggie soon found themselves engrossed in her talk.

"Passover is more than a Jewish Holiday," Dr. Stone began. "It's the story of freedom. Historically, it occurred when the Jews left Egypt, but actually the story is universal. Some of us flee persecution from a government. Some escape a terrible situation such as an abusive marriage. And some of us are physically free, but have taken ourselves prisoners. Others find themselves in a chain gang. What I mean is that sometimes we join up with others who think and live in ways that can harm us. Instead of seeking freedom, we find ourselves living in some kind of communal prison.

"For example, addicts and others with unhealthy habits can egg each other on. That's why when you stop drinking, Alcoholics Anonymous tells you the cold hard truth: that you'll need new friends!

"When you want to lose weight, Weight Watchers urges you to attend the meetings. Your new acquaintances will celebrate your new healthy habits and encourage you to forsake the bad, while a relative or best friend may hand you a piece of fudge cake. Someone who loves you may now become your prison guard.

"Yes, we reinforce each other for the negative as well as the positive. That's because by nature we are social animals and we need each other. So what is a person to do?

"Think of it as your Red Sea crossing. Any change for the good will also have bad moments. How do we offset the despair and dangers of actually moving toward our own freedom land?

"Of course, in the Passover *Haggadah* we learn how G-d intervened to help the Jews enter the Promised Land. But I'm taking tonight's talk beyond Jewish circles, even beyond the spiritual realm, because it's important for each of us to grasp that we are in charge of our own freedom. Leaving the prison of our minds, or the prison of poor choices and decisions is something each of us has to own and do for ourselves.

"Many people of all faiths enjoy the Passover celebration because we all feel uplifted by the end of the social meal after having read the story of how our people were freed from slavery. But let me ask you this: How can we interpret 'next year in Jerusalem' at the end of the *Haggadah* in *personal* terms, rather than in terms of *all* Jews?"

Without hesitation Dr. Stone continued, "one interpretation is that we struggle in our personal freedom to identify who and what are our prisons, and then have to work on taking ourselves to a safer place, a place 'filled with milk and honey' where we can truly be ourselves just as the Jews could be themselves in their own land. And if we can get there by 'next year' then indeed it is worth raising our last cup of wine for the evening as we sit with family and friends at our Passover dinner and all in unison shout out 'next year in Jerusalem!'"

The audience clapped, captivated, and several hands went up signaling the many thoughts to be shared. The lecture ended twenty minutes later. Natalie had taken three pages of notes, intrigued by many of Dr. Stone's concepts. Never before had she connected the holiday to her personal freedom. Previously, it was about her people in ancient time, not her personal self. Dr. Stone brought Passover into the here and now, and Natalie's mind raced as she thought about her own situation. She realized she was in a partial prison, at least as far as her emotions toward the men in her life went, and to some extent, she was also prisoner to her old fears of being deserted. Really being free meant knowing more about what she wanted in life, not just accepting that to which she had become accustomed. But there was even more she definitely wanted to think about later.

Maggie hadn't taken any notes, but she also pondered many of the concepts. She looked back on her marriage as a kind of prison, and was proud of herself for having gotten out and for now engaging in more normal relationships.

Gary was a dear and Raji was unbelievable, but what would she have to do to get back to *her* Jerusalem? First, she wanted to solve the mystery around Chaya Sarah and to help her, if necessary. That was essential. "Thank you, Gary," she smiled at him. "That was really interesting, but let's get out of here so we can learn what you found out today!"

Chapter Twenty

Soon they sat at the diner on 74th Street and Broadway, eating toasted corn muffins and drinking decaf coffee.

"What a great talk," David commented. "My prison is Norwalk Community College. Yet I love being in prison," he laughed.

"I loved the lecture too," Natalie agreed.

"But now we have to get down to business," Maggie asserted. "What did you find out about Chaya Sarah, Gary?"

"Well, actually, nothing, since I don't even have her last name. But I did get some information about the school. I'm assuming you gave me the correct location, of course."

"I did, and anyway it was the only school on that street."

Gary took out his small notebook and opened it. "For one thing, the school is being watched by the authorities and has been for several years. It's large enough for four hundred and fifty kids but only housed one hundred this past year. There were many code violations on record, including vermin and a less-than-adequate sprinkler system. The officer commented that perhaps that was why it was padlocked, although it might also just have been closed for Passover. Many schools in Jerusalem close at least a week before the holiday.

"Apparently, the school has quite a dossier on it, including the implication of being a money laundering operation. Although it's officially owned by a large construction firm, The Dolphin Corporation, with offices in many countries including Jordan, the ownership has always been murky. The firm is known not to be above bribery when it comes to winning a project contract bid. Although government officials have gone to jail for accepting bribes, there has never been enough evidence against the firm to bring major charges. The detective I talked to wondered why in the world a large construction company would want to own a run-down school in a religious neighborhood."

Gary added that although the detective in Jerusalem hadn't researched the kids who attended the school, he commented unofficially to Gary that some of these "different" schools existed for less-than-kosher reasons.

Many of the students there were kids whose parents were either not part of any clear religious community, or were unable to afford the tuition elsewhere.

• • •

"Wow," Maggie and Natalie said practically in unison. "Amazing information," Natalie added.

"So the school has been under surveillance for years. How disturbing!" David looked pointedly at Natalie.

"If the school is owned by a construction company, why wouldn't they take better care of it?" Maggie asked.

"Maybe they only wanted the land," Gary responded.

"What is money laundering, anyway?" Natalie wondered aloud.

"It's complicated, but basically it's a way to move money that was stolen or is otherwise being hidden from the authorities so a company doesn't have to pay any taxes," Gary explained.

"I told you something didn't feel right," David started in again. "Now can you see that whatever the two of you got yourselves into isn't healthy? Who *really* is this Chaya Sarah anyway? If she's so legit, why did she work in that school? There are probably at least one hundred other religious schools in Jerusalem that are totally above suspicion and not under surveillance."

"I have a theory," Maggie replied. "Remember I wrote to you, Gary?"

Gary nodded and smiled. "Yeah, that was quite a theory."

David turned to Maggie. "Okay, let's get everything on the table here. What's your theory?"

Maggie opened up like a flower: "Chaya Sarah was in trouble somehow. Maybe she was born in Jordan and assumed she was Muslim until, at her mother's death bed, she heard her mother say 'Shema' and then her mom whispered with her dying breath that she was Jewish and so was Chaya Sarah. And then Chaya Sarah escaped and came to Jerusalem and studied to be a religious Jew. She was an exceptional scholar and teacher. Over the years she found her way and married a religious man and had a couple of children ..."

"Maggie, your story is even more detailed now," Gary interrupted. "Previously, you suggested she was being pursued by some sort of terrorist group that was putting pressure on her to train terrorists to appear as religious Jews."

"I know, but since then, I think I figured out even more. Let's say some bad guys, like maybe her male cousins, found her and threatened her. They're furious that she now lives as a Jew, but they also see she could be very valuable to them. Either she follows instructions and passes on messages or money, or teaches women how to appear religious. Or they'll hurt her. Maybe her children don't know she grew up Muslim and they threatened to expose her to them. Or maybe they threatened to kidnap her kids and to have them disappear into Jordan or some other Arab land."

"Maggie," Natalie chimed in, "you have the most amazing imagination! I think something isn't quite right, but I don't know what it is. But you have an entire scenario mapped out! What if the school simply closed for Passover?"

"Well, even if that was the case, we know now the school isn't kosher," David replied. "I don't like it. I hope you gals have learned your lesson and will be a little more careful to stay out of harm's way."

Natalie glared at David. "Stop treating us like school girls. Chaya Sarah is wonderful, no matter what the circumstances!"

"Sure," David replied.

They all fell silent, as no one wanted to make the evening worse. Gary and Maggie were newly dating, and manners mattered after all!

Maggie grabbed Gary's hand and gave it a kiss. "Thanks so much for trying so hard to get information for us! It was amazing how quickly you found out stuff."

Gary beamed. The mood softened.

"I'm falling asleep in my decaf," Natalie announced, her way of suggesting they leave.

"By the way," Gary offered as they walked toward Natalie and David's car, "the officer mentioned to me that more and more people are impersonating the very religious. In fact, the city of Jerusalem's police department has set up a major task force to monitor suspects to discover who's behind these efforts."

Though clear that Gary was being thorough and sharing another fact he'd learned from the officer, this last bit of information had a chilling effect on the others.

Maggie feared for Chaya Sarah's safety. Natalie pondered whether Chaya Sarah was as real as she had assumed. She couldn't rule out totally that Chaya Sarah may have been impersonating a religious Jewish woman; ninety-five percent, yes, but one hundred percent, no. Maybe that was her psychological training. People are just too complex to ever be one hundred percent sure. And David? It angered him again that his wife and her best friend had been so naive and foolish as to sit around in some old school's basement, open up their hearts and share their life stories and personal information with a stranger.

Chapter Twenty-One

Natalie could tell David was grumpy as he drove because he constantly changed radio stations. First it was news, then music, then Bloomberg financial information. He always did that when he was in a bad mood. Natalie dozed on and off. She knew it wasn't worth trying to break through his mood. By tomorrow he would be fine. Meanwhile, she needed her own space on her own side of the car.

That night Maggie had the nightmare. She wished she'd written it down when she woke up, so she called Natalie instead. "You have to hear my dream, it was unbelievable! I'm surprised I was able to come up with this intricate a plot. I must be smarter than I thought!"

"Okay, but you'll have to hold on," Natalie cut her off. "I have to get my second cup of coffee . . . okay, I'm back."

"Here goes," Maggie launched. "It was really dark out in the dream, as if there was a storm coming any minute. The sky was black with clouds and the wind was blowing. A woman who looked like Chaya Sarah was running quickly across a field, as if she was being chased. Then she was in an old-fashioned town. It looked kind of like a town from the Wild West in old cowboy movies, but I knew it was supposed to be a shtetl somewhere in Poland. I don't know how I knew that, but I did. Then there was a wild boar running down the center of the street, out of control. A wagon drawn by a horse flipped over as the boar came through, and there was chaos in the street. Then everything changed and some menacing men came toward a cave where I was hiding. They searched everywhere, and I knew they would find me. Just then I woke up. Huh! The dream doesn't sound as fascinating as I thought it was. I guess I'm not that brilliant. But it did wake me up and leave me with my heart pounding."

"It's okay. I love you, even if you aren't brilliant," Natalie chuckled. "I guess Gary's information somehow got turned around in your head as you slept, and you ended up having an old fashioned nightmare. I actually slept like a log. I guess I just needed the sleep."

"Natalie, you haven't said anything since we've been back and I'm wondering. Are you in touch with Jack?"

"I hadn't heard a word from him until this morning. In fact, I was going to call you. You just beat me to the phone."

"Well, what did he say?"

"Not much. Just that he's busy going back and forth to London and that he misses me. He said just enough to stir up feelings I don't want to have stirred up."

"Might I remind you that he has a wife and three children?"

"Thanks for the information."

"Might I also remind you that David is very much in love with you?"

"Okay, enough! I have to work all this through. Platitudes and facts are not going to solve the issue of old feelings coming back to life."

"Oh, excuse me, miss, or should I say, Dr. Psychologist. I'm just an ordinary person who happens to remember what a jerk Jack was years ago. My mother always said that people don't really change. I should have believed her when she told me that my ex was not to be trusted. But no! I had to see for myself…for twenty miserable years."

"It's true that we don't change much. But sometimes it's just a tiny shift that makes a person better."

"If he were a better person, he would leave you alone. You have a wonderful husband, and Jack is aware of that."

"Well, I still need to get past some of these intense feelings. Tonight I'm making a nice dinner for David and we're just going to relax. Believe me I'm going to try as hard as possible to just focus on him."

"Good girl! Talk to you tomorrow." As Maggie hung up the phone she realized she'd been kind of tough on Natalie. After all, she was also involved with two men and felt entitled to be. But a nagging feeling began to appear that she wasn't so comfortable about and that she hadn't bothered to share with Natalie. She missed the "romance of a stranger" that she had experienced with Raji for those couple of glorious days. There was no way in the world that Gary could come close to that type of international flavor. She thought of Raji and imagined him slowly and sensuously removing the brilliant orange sari with gold and silver trim that she would be wearing. When she thought of Gary, she wondered only if the police officer in Jerusalem had gotten back to him again. There was a big difference between where her mind and heart traveled!

And as far as sleeping with Gary she hadn't been able to bring herself to do so again. She was beginning to get the feeling that it wasn't so easy to sleep with two different guys.

This could turn into a bit of a mess! She could hold Gary off only a little while longer. Would she end up sleeping with two men at once? Was that any worse than Natalie struggling with a possible affair with Jack? And what about Chaya Sarah? Who would be there to help her? Who would free her if she was caught in some awful scenario of mystery and terrorism? Maggie felt her palms begin to sweat and her heartbeat quicken. She had a strange feeling that the best and the worst were yet to come.

Be Sure To Find Out in Part 3 of
Next Year in Jerusalem!

About the Author

DR. BARBARA BECKER HOLSTEIN, internationally known positive psychologist, inspires thousands with her ENCHANTED SELF®. Around the world people benefit from her techniques to enhance well-being, and to live up to their potential. Known for her ability to make complex psychological concepts easy to understand and to implement, she has now turned her talents to novel writing. "A great fiction read is a great escape, and yet, it is more! It is the gateway to new ways of thinking and behaving."

She received her Doctorate in Education from Boston University and her BA degree from Barnard College. Dr. Holstein has been a school psychologist and taught first and second grades. She is in private practice with her husband, Dr. Russell M. Holstein, in Long Branch, New Jersey.

She can be found on the web at:
www.EnchantedSelf.com
www.TheTruthForGirls.com
www.Next-Year-in-Jerusalem.com
www.NewRomanceBooks.com.

A partial listing of her books includes:
- THE ENCHANTED SELF: *A Positive Therapy*
- *Recipes for Enchantment: The Secret Ingredient is You!*
- *The Truth (I'm a girl, I'm smart and I know everything)*
- *Seven Gateways to Happiness: Freeing Your Enchanted Self*